A SINISTER SIGN

LIZZIE ~ THE PREQUEL

THE WESTPORT ROMANTIC MYSTERIES

BETH PRENTICE

BOOKS BY BETH PRENTICE

The Westport Romantic Mysteries

Lizzie

A Sinister Sign ~ The Prequel

Dangerous Deeds

Give Murder A Hand

Deathly Desire

The Christmas Gift – A Mini Lizzie Mystery

Molly

Wicked Little Lies

Gracie

The Ivory Veil – a novella

Chloe

Killer Unleashed

Deadly Tails

Alexandra

Invitation to Murder

The Aloha Lagoon Samantha Reynolds Mysteries

Deadly Wipeout

Lethal Tide

Fatal Break

Tidal Wave

The Dandelion Ponds Mysteries

In High Spirits

The Hollyday Spirit - novella

That's the Spirit

The Dun Roamin' Romantic Mysteries

Tilly ~ Before Dun Roamin'

Matilda's Wish

CHAPTER 1

"Are you sure about this, Lizzie?" My brother, Danny, placed his hands on his hips and screwed up his nose as he stared at the building in front of us.

I followed his gaze, noting the window shutter dangling precariously by a single hinge. The paint was peeling, the garden was overgrown, and the roof looked like it might collapse at any moment. But if you squinted your eyes, tilted your head and looked past all that, you could see the beauty it had once been.

"Yes. I'm certain. The house is stunning."

Danny's jaw dropped faster than my savings account balance during a Black Friday sale. "Are we looking at the same building?" His voice was three octaves higher than normal.

As a hairdresser, Danny usually worked on a Saturday, but he'd taken some time off between clients to accompany me to an open inspection of a house I was considering purchasing. It was a great idea at the time, but now I was thinking I should have come alone.

"Yes! Just wait until you see inside," I gushed. "It's got the most amazing bay windows, and from upstairs you can even see the river." An unfamiliar warm feeling burned bright inside my chest.

Glancing around, I crossed my fingers and hoped I was the only serious buyer and the ten other people meandering around the grounds would just shake their heads and go home. Well… in fairness, some of them were doing just that.

The auction was in a few days' time, and to say I was nervous was an understatement. I'd never purchased a house before, and I'd never been to an auction. Danny had promised he would come along and help me with the bidding, but as he sneered at the property, I figured he'd rather sit on me and keep me at home until the auction was over.

"Come on," I said. "You'll soon see what I'm talking about."

I ignored the dubious lift of his eyebrows and grabbed the arm of his shawl-neck sweater, pulling him onto the graveled driveway.

"Watch the clothing," he warned, gently yet firmly removing my hand. "It's new. In fact, hang on a moment. I'm going to leave it in the car for fear of anything happening to it in that, that…"

"House," I finished for him, rolling my eyes.

"If you say so."

I sighed but refused to allow him to dampen my enthusiasm. "Danny, if you leave your sweater in the car, you'll freeze."

"Better option than risking anything happening to it. Maybe you should…" He looked me up and down before shaking his head. "No, don't worry."

"What?"

"I was going to suggest you do the same, but…" He screwed up his nose again, as he squinted.

"You know if you keep doing that, you'll get wrinkles, right?"

He gasped as his hand shot to his temple, and I watched as he felt around for any creases that may have appeared in the last few minutes.

I hid my grin before hurriedly assessing my outfit. The jacket was a hand-me-down from our sister, Molly. It was denim, frayed at the cuffs, and had faded in patches until it was almost white, but it was comfortable, and I loved it.

"What's wrong with what I'm wearing?"

"Four years ago, the jacket was divine, but I would never pair it with those overalls. Denim on denim is just a bit too matchy-matchy, if you know what I mean."

No, I didn't know what he meant. Instead, I threw my hands in the air and watched him march to his car.

Danny was one of the nicest humans I knew. He was kind, considerate, and would do anything to help you, but when it came to fashion, he was ruthless.

I silently admitted that his black skinny jeans and Calvin Klein T-shirt looked great under that sweater. And I loved how he had added a red streak through the side fringe he'd slicked down over his left ear before straightening the rest of his short hair. Like me, Danny struggled with his curls.

However, I chose to allow nature to fly free, rarely having the patience to fight with the hair straightener. Instead, I tied my long dark locks into a ponytail and allowed the humidity to do its thing. I may not look as classy as my siblings, but I had a heck of a lot more free time on my hands.

Tightening the band holding my frizz off my neck, I scanned my surroundings for anyone who looked like a potential buyer and not just a lookie-loo. The open house event was extremely busy. Cars lined the otherwise quiet street as groups wandered the grounds. Two couples were jostling for pole position heading for the agent stationed at the front door, and I tapped my foot impatiently until Danny hurried back and we joined them.

"Happy now?" I asked, watching him rub the goose bumps from his arms.

"Not really, but it will have to do."

I released a slow breath as he walked ahead of me, his Italian leather loafers crunching the gravel beneath his feet as we made our way toward the front door.

"Lizzie, why don't you buy one of those new houses over near the horse track? Andrew and I looked at them last week, and they are soooo cute!"

"Because the lights from the night races would keep me awake."

Danny spun to face me, his eyes wide. "You sleep like the dead! How are a few little lights going to annoy you?"

"They're not little. They're huge. And I'll have you know that I'm a light sleeper."

"Since when?"

"Since living in the city for ten years. I'd hear even the tiny squeak of a mouse." That wasn't strictly true, but I didn't need to give Danny anymore fuel for his argument.

His snort told me he didn't believe me, but thankfully he bit his tongue on his retort as we joined the queue.

"Geez, why do so many people want to get into this dump?" Danny asked.

I was about to point out the gorgeous molding around the doorframe when the lady in front of us leaned toward her partner and whispered loud enough for us to hear. "How much to knock it down and clear the land?"

Danny choked on his laugh as he nudged my shoulder.

"You just have no imagination," I replied indignantly.

Thankfully he chose to remain quiet as we patiently waited our turn to enter the hallway. Okay, I wasn't that patient, but I did my best. Butterflies zipped in my belly as I fiddled with my thin bangle and bounced on the balls of my feet.

"Good morning." The middle-aged Realtor greeted us once the demolition couple had stepped inside. "Welcome to number three May Street." His blue shirt had sweat marks under the arms, his tie was loosened at the collar, and his name badge told me he was "Bob."

"Is this your first time visiting us here?" He handed me a

brochure professing the benefits of living in this old house. He needn't have bothered. I was already in love with it.

"I had an inspection last week, but another agent was here then," I explained, giving Bob my full attention.

"Ah, that would have been Zachary. Unfortunately, he was in a terrible accident and needs some time off work, so I'm taking over for him."

I gasped. "Is he okay? He was really nice. He told me all about the house and how it's been owned by the same family for generations and how it's now being sold as part of a decedent's estate, which is really sad. But at the same time I'm thrilled I get a chance to buy it. Oh, and he also told me all personal effects including furniture have already been sold, so it's empty. But that's okay, as I've got a good imagination and can visualize what it will look like furnished." It all came out in a rush and left me slightly lightheaded.

Bob stared back at me, his eyes wide. "Yes, yes. Well, Zac seems to have given you the rundown then. And he'll be fine. He's quite clumsy, and it seems he was upstairs closing the window and he fell."

"Out the window?" My jaw dropped, and I smacked my lips with my hand.

"Yes. But don't worry," Bob hurriedly added, his palm in the halt position. "That side of the house is quite overgrown, and the shrubs broke his fall."

Danny sucked in a breath as a passer-by mumbled something about the house being cursed.

Bob glared after them. "It's quirky, not damned," he muttered before his gaze flicked back to me. "Please pay them no attention. Now, may I have your name for our records?" His finger poised over the screen of his electronic tablet.

"Lizzie Fuller. And this is my brother, Danny."

"And you're the purchaser, Lizzie?"

"Ahuh."

Bob's index finger moved at lightning speed as he entered my name into his database.

"Excuse me for interrupting." A woman stepped up behind him and tapped him on the shoulder. Her long caramel-colored tresses were tied at her neck, perspiration beaded around her hairline, and the jacket of her Westport Property Sales uniform looked constricting. "I was wondering if I could have a quick word?" I detected a distinct tremble in her voice, as she gave me a friendly, albeit distracted smile.

"I'm sorry, Bianca, but I'm a little busy." Bob chuckled, yet his lips pulled in a tight line as he considered her.

"It's just that…" She leaned in and whispered in his ear. They were quiet, but the words *haunted* and *scary* definitely drifted my way.

"Not now!" Bob hissed under his breath.

He then turned to me, his smile as fake as his tan. "Please go ahead and look around. I can get the rest of your details on the way out."

Poor Bianca. I was about to suggest that Thompson's Smash Repairs was looking for a new receptionist when I stepped forward and tripped, falling into Bob. My hand reached for anything to stop me, and I palm-slapped his tablet straight into his nose.

Bianca snorted but hurriedly covered it with a cough. I mumbled my apologies and scurried past them, choosing to avoid eye contact with Bob.

"Good first impression, Lizzie." Danny chuckled, dragging me away as fast as he could.

"At least I'll be memorable." There was always an upside.

The temperature in the foyer rose a few degrees, packed with bodies all surveying the uneven floor and faded wallpaper. Words like *demolition*, and *not worth restoring*, and *perfect development site* filtered into my brain causing my breathing to accelerate. I'd swear my belly butterflies were auditioning for *Cirque Du Soleil*. A woman with glacial blue eyes gave me the once over before looking down her nose, but I took a calming breath and pushed past her in the hallway, heading up the stairs.

I knew once Danny saw the view from the master bedroom, and I explained the plans I had for the tiny attic space, he'd be as enchanted as I was.

Entering the room, I ignored the small crowd eyeing a suspicious stain on the carpet and pulled my phone out of my shoulder bag. Opening Google images, I showed Danny my inspiration for the makeover.

"I thought in here, I could polish the floorboards and paint the walls. I love the deep skirting boards and the high ceilings, and just look at that ornate plaster around the light." A deep, contented sigh escaped my lips as I glanced around the room.

"It's more of a dim bulb dangling from a dodgy electrical cord." Danny's shoulders slumped and a deep crease appeared between his brows.

"You have to look past that bit. See the beauty this can become."

Danny stepped away from me mumbling something about the electrical burning the house down, but I tuned him out, wishing I'd brought Grandma Mabel with me instead. She loved adventures and would have been a whole lot more excited about what this house could become.

"Oh my God!" Danny screamed, leaning out the window.

I thought, like Zac, he was falling, and raced across the room. In my haste, I bumped into a man with an earring and a crooked nose who stood with his hands on his hips glaring at everyone in turn. A scar ran from his lip to his chin, and I shivered as a chill raced down my spine. Boy, was I glad it was broad daylight, and I wasn't meeting him in a dark alley.

"Sorry," I mumbled. "So sorry."

He sneered, and I hurried to put some space between us.

"Danny! What's wrong?" I grabbed the back of his shirt, hoping to keep him safe.

"Oh my God, Lizzie. You should see this guy wandering around the garden. I think it's Adonis." Danny fanned himself as he leaned farther over the ledge, his eyes wide.

"What? Are you kidding me? I thought you were falling!" I yelled a little bit louder than intended, and the man with the scar glared at me.

But then again, I could have earned that glare from knocking his brochure out of his hand. As he leaned down to pick it up, his dark eyes locked onto mine.

Oh geez. Luckily, I had a strong pelvic floor, otherwise I may have peed my pants. Actually…urgh!

I cringed and hurriedly turned my attention to Danny, hoping the guy would just move on, simultaneously wondering where the nearest usable bathroom was.

"If I fell, do you think Adonis would catch me?" Danny grinned, his eyes twinkling with mischief. A lot of good-looking men caught his attention, but few gained that reaction.

"Remember your partner, Andrew? The one who loves you, cooks for you, and puts up with your crap?"

Danny gawked at me, his hands on his hips. "You need to lighten up more. Now hurry up. You're going to miss him, and you'll be sorry."

I rolled my eyes but gazed out the window, just in time to see the back of a tall, blond guy. From what I could see, I had to admit that Danny had good taste in men.

The man appeared to be inspecting the front porch, and as he moved his cotton shirt stretched across his back outlining more muscle than I had seen in quite some time. His jeans rode low on his narrow hips, and toned arms pushed on rotting timber before he stood and disappeared around the corner. Geez, if his back looked that good, what did his front look like?

I licked my dry lips and turned to Danny. "He's gone."

"*What?* Where did he go?" Pushing me aside he leaned over the window ledge. I made a mental note that if I purchased the house, I would have to get some screens made. If that opening was big enough for Danny, then it was big enough for a spider. And a spider in my bedroom was definitely not something on my wish list.

No, but Adonis would be a nice addition.

I gasped at my unwelcome thoughts. I had a boyfriend and despite the fact that his back didn't look anywhere near that sexy, he was mine. And that was all I needed. Right?

"Come on. You need to show me the outside," Danny called, dodging *scar man* as he scurried toward the hallway.

"I didn't know you liked gardens that much."

"I don't. But I'm hoping Adonis does, and I can get a close-up look at him."

As appealing as that sounded, I pulled my shoulders back and stayed strong.

"But I want to show you the attic first," I whined, bustling after him.

"Lizzie. Attics can wait."

"You have a partner, Danny. You shouldn't be looking at other men." Words I usually lived by.

"I know. But that doesn't stop you from looking."

"Ah, yes, it does. Remember Scott?" My throat thickened as I remembered my boyfriend and how my thoughts about the man in the garden had betrayed him.

Danny stopped short on the landing and wrinkled his nose. "Oh yeah. How did I forget about him?"

I huffed at his lack of enthusiasm. I'd always known Scott didn't really fit with my family, but that didn't mean Danny had to dismiss him the way he did. Choosing not to reply, I ignored the twinge in my stomach, refocused, and headed for the second set of stairs, making my way to the attic, my phone filled with dreams for what it could become.

As a bookkeeper for *Bradley and Sons Accountants*, I'd loved the thrill of living in a busy city, where it was constantly exciting and full of life. But in the past twelve months I'd yearned for a quieter lifestyle, to move home to the town I'd grown up in and to my family. So I'd made arrangements with my boss to work from home, and since the city was only half an hour away by car, I could just pop into the office whenever I needed to…

… which brought me to the room now in front of me. The tiny attic space would make the perfect office. With its Dormer window and angled ceilings, it gave me the character I had craved while sharing a modern two-bedroom flat with my friend Aimee.

I could envision where my desk would sit and how I would separate the space to accommodate a storeroom and maybe a tiny bathroom up here.

Lost in my daydreams, I almost didn't notice the two women who had moved in behind me.

"I'm going to see if they'll accept an offer prior to the auction." The petite woman flicked her fire engine red curls over her shoulder and smiled at the brunette next to her.

My heart sank. I didn't know you could do that.

"I'd do it quickly if I were you," replied the brunette. "Did you see the guy in the suit staring at every other prospective buyer? If you're not quick, I reckon he'll beat you to it."

"Who was he? It's not common to see designer suits in Westport."

"I overheard him telling Bob he was an agent representing a buyer who wished to keep their identity quiet."

Well, that was intriguing.

"Whoever the buyer is must have money," the redhead mused.

"Yep. That's what I thought too. He sounds like a developer, and I reckon he'll snap this place up, knock it down, and either build apartments or sell the land for a quick profit."

"To be fair, I'd knock it down too. Only I'd build my dream

home on the site. Did you see the view from the master bedroom? You could build an amazing home here."

The petite woman glanced at me and gave a weak smile.

"You'd better chat to the agent now, then," prompted her friend before they both turned and hurried back the way they came.

I moved to the window seat and sank down onto it, aimlessly staring outside, smoothing the cool sides of my phone for comfort.

I'd never fallen in love with a property before, but I'd fallen hard for this one. I barely noticed the faded wallpaper, the rotting architraves, or even the water damage to the ceiling. All I could see was what it could become and how I could build my new life here. I could bring the life back to the house that it deserved. I had no idea what kind of family had lived here, but I believed houses absorbed their feelings. It had witnessed them grow, standing proud over them and keeping them safe. It didn't deserve to end its life as scrap timber. Nope, it needed to be restored, to be loved once again, and to live with a new family under its roof, filling it with happy memories.

With a renewed energy I stood, pulled my shoulders back and marched downstairs to find Bob.

A HARSH-LOOKING lady with short dark hair pushed her thick glasses up the bridge of her beaky nose and glared at Bob. "It needs a lot of work." She tutted.

"And that will reflect in the price, Hazel," he announced as he dabbed the perspiration from his lip.

"What's the price range?" she asked.

"I'm not legally allowed to divulge that. However, if you register for the auction, I'm sure you will be happy with the result."

"Oh, I don't think so. I'm more interested in who will purchase it. This is a lovely street. We don't need any riffraff moving in and spoiling it."

"Even more of a reason to purchase it yourself," Bob coaxed.

I shuffled from one foot to the other and wished he'd just shut up. The fewer bidders the better in my opinion.

"You could quite possibly be right." Hazel tapped her lip as the man with the scar bumped her shoulder, making his way out the front door.

I sucked in a breath, glad it wasn't me. Even though the look he threw my way made me wonder if he'd actually been aiming for me.

"Excuse me!" She huffed and marched after him, obviously unafraid of the dark aura he projected. "That was very rude. You should apologize."

I silently thanked *scar man* for one: leaving, and two: making Hazel leave Bob's side and giving me the chance I needed to talk to him.

"Ah, Lizzie, wasn't it?"

"That's me," I trilled.

"Do you have any questions I can answer?"

"Yes. Will you accept my offer today?"

Bob laughed. "You're keen."

"I've kind of fallen in love with the house."

Danny stepped up behind me and kicked my shoe, his code for *Shut up, Lizzie*. In hindsight, I guess it wasn't smart to tell the agent how enthusiastic I was if I wanted to keep the price down.

"Good, good. That's what we like to hear. Unfortunately, there's a lot of interest in the house, and the seller's solicitor thinks it's in their best interest for it to go to auction."

Disappointment weighed heavy in my stomach. "I guess that means the lady with the red hair can't buy it yet either then?"

"No. I can tell you that there will be some stiff competition on auction day, so come prepared. Have your finances organized prior, and if you'd like a building inspection done, it needs to be completed before Monday at five o'clock. That doesn't leave you a lot of time."

"Zac didn't mention that to me." I bit my lip, thinking about what options I had.

"Did he give you a package on the property? All the information and bidder registration documents were in there."

I nodded but didn't admit I hadn't actually read the information. I'd been too caught up with my dream of what the house could become. In hindsight, I would have been better off doing my homework rather than whittling away the hours on the internet, but hindsight is a wonderful thing.

"Can I get a building inspection this afternoon?" I asked, my breath bottling in my chest.

Bob checked his watch. "Considering that it's nearly four o'clock on Friday, I highly doubt it."

Oh.

Danny beamed, seemingly happy that this could be the stumbling block he needed.

My shoulders sank as I stepped out onto the tiny front porch. It groaned under my weight, but then that could have been me.

"Come on, Lizzie. Let's go and grab a coffee, and I'll show you those new builds over near the racetrack."

The problem was the new builds didn't stir the feelings of excitement this house did. Buying a home was a big decision that should be made with my head not my heart, but one thing I knew about myself was my heart never had it wrong. When I listened to it and didn't question what it was feeling, my heart only led me to great things.

Stepping onto the dead grass and looking back at the house I took a deep breath and closed my eyes, listening to my emotions.

Buy the house. You know it's the right thing to do.

But what about the hard work and money it's going to take?

Don't worry about that. It will all work itself out with time.

Remember there's no such thing as a bad decision. There's only a decision.

Snapping my lids open, I grinned before releasing a deep contented sigh. Bugger the building inspection. I mean, what could it tell me that I couldn't see already?

I took a step toward Bob, ready to complete the bidder registration, when the sound of a motor revving and tires screeching filled the air. I turned to look at the road just in time to see a black car with dark tinted windows peel away from the curb, accelerating down the street and heading straight for the petite redhead who had just stepped into the road.

My breath stilled, and the world slowed as she stared at the vehicle. Her screams were drowned by the roaring of the engine. Her hands rose to cover her face, her feet seemingly glued to the road.

My own heart raced as the desire to run and help her overwhelmed me. But time wasn't on my side.

As her friend screamed for the car to stop, the echo of the sickening thud filled the air, before the car disappeared down the street, the driver not even hesitating in his getaway.

CHAPTER 2

The rest of the afternoon was all a bit of a blur. There were a lot of red and blue flashing lights, a lot of questions fired at me by the police, and a lot of onlookers including WTN News. One of Westport's more famous reporters had tried to interview me, but it seemed in times of stress I was a bumbling idiot. He quickly moved to Danny who lapped up the limelight, despite not actually having seen what had happened.

We were presently sitting around the table at our parents' house, and I was devouring one of Mum's double chocolate cupcakes like there was no tomorrow—which apparently was going to be the case for the petite redhead. According to one onlooker, the second her head hit the road the world had lost her.

Sadness for her family and friends sat heavy in my chest, and a thousand *if onlys* ran through my mind. If only she hadn't been there at that moment in time. If only the driver of the car that hit her had been paying more attention. If only I had noticed the license plate of the car.

"Lizzie, no one saw the plate," snapped Danny, seemingly reading my mind. "According to one lady the car had no plates."

"It had to have had them," added our sister Molly, flicking her long dark curls over her shoulder before dabbing a stray crumb from her pink painted lips. As always Molly looked exceptional. Her tight black T-shirt was cut just low enough to show off her double Ds. Her sleek curls shone under the overhead florescent light, and her long eyelashes reflected her inner beauty. "It's illegal not to."

Danny shrugged, Mum tutted, and Grandma Mabel swished her false teeth around.

Friday night was usually a time my siblings and I hung out together. However, Sunday dinner with Mum and Dad had been moved forward as they had been invited to Grandma Carol's. Danny, Molly, and I all preferred to avoid her as much as possible, so we agreed to the date change.

"What's Westport coming to?" mused Mum, smearing cream onto the tiramisu we were having for dessert.

"Back in my day, the driver would have stopped to help the poor woman," added Grandma Mabel picking a piece of dropped cake off her sparkly pink shirt. The T-shirt was as loose as her skin, and its color matched her curls.

"Maybe they didn't see her. No one intentionally runs someone down." Danny's partner, Andrew, was seventeen years older than Danny and was always the calming influence on our group.

"Then why didn't they stop?" I chewed my lip as silence descended.

"That house has bad karma," said Mum breaking into my thoughts. "You need to stay away from it, Lizzie." She hit me with a stare that was designed to make me run for cover. Growing up it had worked every time. Apparently, it still worked on me today.

"Don't be silly, Nelle," warned Grandma Mabel. "It's not the house's fault that someone doesn't know how to drive."

And that's why Grandma Mabel was my favorite.

"I'm not saying it is. I'm just saying there's bad karma there.

Lizzie would be far better off buying one of those new builds behind us."

It was Molly's turn to hit me with a glare. Only this glare told me to run from Mum's idea. "Well, I think Lizzie would be better off looking at the new apartments they've built alongside the river. They're spectacular."

"And a good ten minutes from here," Danny whispered under his breath.

"But if she lived behind us, we'd always be there to help her," added Mum, cream dripping from the spoon as her hand froze over the cake.

"Nelle, Lizzie is thirty-one years old. She's a grown woman who can take care of herself. Let her live wherever she wants to." Grandma swished her teeth around one more time before turning her attention to the cupcakes.

Mum once again tutted before swatting Grandma's hand with the spoon. "No one is going to want to eat their dinner at this rate."

I couldn't answer for the others, but I for one intended to at least stay for dessert. It looked delicious.

"Where's Dad?" I asked, picking at the last of the crumbs on my plate.

"He's been held up at the Men's Shed."

"What?" yelled Grandma. "How? Why didn't you mention this earlier? Are the police there?"

We all turned to her, the vertical lines between each of our brows identical.

"Grandma, what are you talking about?" asked Danny.

"Nelle just said he was held up!"

"Yes. He's been held up because Jimmy Tennent needed some help with the lathe. What did you think I meant?"

Grandma's bottom dentures popped out from behind her lip as her cheeks reddened. "Oh. Well, that's not very exciting," she mumbled.

"Why don't you have a lie-down before dinner?" Mum suggested.

"That might be a good idea. Eunice is coming by later, and we're going to that new place in town. What's it called?"

We all shrugged.

"You know the place, Molly. You went there last weekend," Grandma prompted.

"Do you mean the Scotch Bar?"

"That's the one. You said the bartender was really cute. Eunice and I thought we'd go and check it out, see if we concur with your opinion."

"Grandma, it's Friday night. The place will be packed."

"Even better. I was going to wear the dress I found at the thrift shop yesterday. It's almost brand new. Except for the ink stain on the pocket, there's barely a mark on it. And when I pair it with those new shoes I got from the podiatrist, no one's going to be looking at my pockets."

I'd seen the shoes and knew she was one hundred percent correct about that.

"Sounds nice," I commented, noting the way both Danny and Molly recoiled at the idea of purchasing preloved clothing. "What's the dress like?"

"Oh, Lizzie, it's glorious. It's bright yellow with green llamas all over it and a lovely trim of tulle popping out showing off my knees."

"You're not going out in that?" Mum's mouth formed an O as her eyes widened. I wasn't sure if she was more frightened by the fact that Grandma and her bestie were spending the evening at the hottest club in town or by the fact she was wearing the dress.

"I sure am. I've got great knees, and they deserve to be shown off. Wait till Eunice sees me. She's going to be green with envy."

I was almost certain Mum whispered something along the lines of, "She'll be green all right," But I could have misheard as when I glanced at Mum, her lips were clamped shut.

Grandma stood and moved to her purple wheelie walker, pushing it ahead of her as she shuffled her way to her bedroom.

Once upon a time Grandma had lived independently, but after she set the oven on fire, my mum and dad decided it was best she live with them.

I'd like to say it was an arrangement made in heaven, but more honestly, it was an experiment in tolerance. Grandma and Mum were like chalk and cheese. Grandma was the fiery wild one, while Mum was the sensible stable one. The upside to the arrangement was that Mum baked when she was stressed, and I loved cake. So, if you asked my opinion on their living arrangement, I leaned toward the heaven camp, whereas I was sure Dad leaned more toward the hell camp. But it was working. Kind of.

"You have to stop her," Mum hissed to Molly once Grandma was out of earshot.

"Why?"

"Because it was your fault she even heard of the Scotch Bar."

"She would have heard of it without me. I've dropped her at Bingo, and I know how quickly news spreads in that place."

Mum's shoulders sagged as she stood and collected a container of un-iced cupcakes.

"Why me?" she whispered, as she placed the chocolate delights on the table. I noted her silently counting them before her lips pursed and her gaze swept the table.

You see, there had been twelve cakes, but I may have eaten one. Okay, I'd eaten two, but let's not point that out. They were supposed to be for us to take home later, and I knew Molly would complain if she didn't get her share.

"So, the house auction is on Monday..." I said to Mum, hurriedly moving the conversation in a different direction. Only as a tick started under her eye, and her gaze fell to me, I wasn't sure if this was the direction I wanted to head.

AFTER DINNER, I kissed my family, bid my good nights, and then headed to Molly's. I no longer had a place to call home as the second I had told my friend Aimee I was moving out, she had sublet my room to one of her university friends, and he needed the room ASAP. It hadn't bothered me too much except for the fact that my worldly possessions were now stacked in Dad's garage, and I had no idea where my hair straightener was. Like I said, it didn't bother me too much.

Molly had left ahead of me, needing to stop at a fuel station before heading home. That gave me some time to myself, and it didn't take long for me to point my little Mini Cooper in the direction of the old house on May Street. No matter how hard I tried, I couldn't stop thinking about it. It filled my soul with a desire I had never encountered before, and I was determined to be the new owner.

Making my way across town, I noted the large jacarandas had dropped their leaves, their bare branches stretching up into the darkness as the streetlights flashed over my windshield. Westport wasn't the largest town on the east coast. The last census said it had a population of thirty thousand. It had one large hospital, one cemetery and one shopping center. It was everything I needed, and a warm fuzzy feeling sat low in my belly with the knowledge I was moving home.

I smiled, blissfully aware of how quiet the streets were. Blinds had been lowered, curtains were pulled, and I wound my window down to enjoy the evening scent of winter filling the air.

Pulling up to the curb at number three, I stopped behind a silver four-wheel drive advertising *Westport Property Sales* and killed the motor. The only sign of the earlier accident were the lines drawn on the road by the police. A cold breeze surrounded me, and I shuddered as I leaned forward, my gaze moving to the house. A light burned bright in one of the upstairs windows.

Hmmm, was Bob doing a private viewing for someone? If so, maybe I could sneak in for a second look. I did want to measure the master bedroom to see if my king-size bed would fit after all, and this would give me the opportunity before the auction on Monday.

Without a second thought, I hurriedly pushed the car door open and jogged toward the house, hoping to catch Bob before he locked up.

A chill ran down my spine as I negotiated the dark driveway, causing me to pull my jacket tightly around me. Westport's winters were never fierce, but as the westerly winds whipped, I was grateful spring was only a few weeks away.

Bob's voice boomed from the open door as I negotiated the path. Suddenly, the overgrown bushes under the front window rustled, and a woman tumbled out of them. My heart rate spiked.

"This danged house!" she cursed, rolling onto her side, and I immediately recognized Hazel, the nosy neighbor.

"Oh! You scared me," I called, placing my hand on my heart. "Are you all right?"

"Of course I'm all right," she snapped, getting to her feet before I could offer a hand.

"What were you doing?"

"Oh, well I… umm… just wanted to check on something."

"In the bushes?"

"What? No! I just… never mind. It's none of your business what I was doing."

Bob's loud voice startled me once again.

"Lizzie? What are you doing here?" His dark brow furrowed, as he held his phone in his hand.

"Oh, hi, Bob." I gave him a two-finger wave. "I was just driving past and saw the light on. I was hoping to have a quick look around."

He stood back and motioned for me to enter the foyer. "I'll just be a minute," he said before returning to his call. "Sorry for the interruption. You were saying?"

A deep, sexy voice echoed from the speaker, and my mind

jumped to the man I'd seen in the garden earlier that day. "I'd love to bid on the house, but I've been called out of town for work, and now I can't make the auction on Monday." The rich baritone of the caller's voice caused goosebumps to break-dance over my skin, and a delicious involuntary shiver rippled down my spine. I'd never been one to listen to meditation apps, but if that caller was the voice on the other end of my headphones, I'd be more Zen than the Dalai Lama.

Bob hummed and ahhed a few times before saying, "I'm so sorry that you won't be able to make the auction, but we will accept a phone bid if that would work for you."

A long sigh echoed through the speaker. "I won't have any phone signal."

"Then you could get someone to bid on your behalf."

I gasped at the idea of another bidder, causing Bob to narrow his eyes in my direction before turning his back to me.

"Maybe. I'll talk to my dad, and see if he's able to make it," the caller replied. "Are you sure the vendor won't accept a prior offer?"

"Sorry, Riley, but that's a definite no. Believe you me, I've asked."

"Okay. Thanks, Bob. I'll see what I can work out."

Hmmm, that didn't bode well for me. My budget was limited, and I needed cash to do the renovations, which meant I needed to get the house at the cheapest price possible. The more bidders, the higher the price. I said a silent prayer that the owner of the sexy voice wouldn't be able to get anyone to do his bidding for him.

Bob gave the obligatory goodbyes before ending the call and turning to me.

"If I had a dollar for every person who wanted to make an offer prior to auction, I'd be a rich man." He ran his hand through his hair, and the dismal overhead lighting accentuated the dark rings under his eyes.

"I didn't expect you to be here at this time," I commented. Even though I was very happy that he was.

"No. Well, I shouldn't be here, but I had a prospective buyer adamant that she needed a viewing before Monday's auction." His eyes rolled to the ceiling at the sound of high heels clicking against a timber floor. "I explained that the house will be open for inspection for an hour prior to auction, but apparently she couldn't wait until then. Now, may I ask what I can do for you?"

"Oh, well, I too was hoping to have a sneaky look." I grinned as Bob released a self-suffering sigh. "I mean, the house is open, and I will only be a minute. I just wanted to measure up for the bed."

Judging by the glee that pushed Bob's frustration aside, I figured he liked the idea of a bidding war. "If you must," he replied, his hand sweeping toward the stairs.

I stifled an excited squeal and headed upward, as Bob answered another call. It seemed the life of a real estate agent was never quiet. "Hello. Oh! What do you want?... Look I've already told you..."

His voice drifted into background noise as the boards creaked and groaned with every step I took. Three-quarters of the way up, the tread gave way and slipped out from under me. I screamed, threw my hands out in an effort to slow my fall, and landed with a clunk, my nose hitting the black patent leather of a gorgeous pair of Louboutins.

"Bugger!" I cursed, scrambling to sit up, rubbing my nose in the process.

"Are you kidding me?" The owner of the shoes was an elegant blonde woman. And she didn't look impressed with my nose print on her shoes.

"Sorry. So sorry." I reached out and used my sleeve to wipe the shiny shoes clean.

The blonde snatched her foot away and glared at me. Shaking

her head, she marched down the stairs without even a backward glance to see if I was okay.

I sighed, even more determined to win the auction.

Regaining my composure, I made my way across the landing. The old Victorian house plan was pretty simple. Downstairs there was a main hallway with the staircase off the front door. To the right of the stairs was the lounge room and to the left was the kitchen. It was the same on the second floor, only to the right was the master bedroom and to the left was the bathroom. Off the landing was a second set of stairs leading to the attic.

I ducked past those and headed for the master bedroom as the voices of Bob and the blonde drifted up toward me. She was professing the benefits of bulldozing the house, and Bob was agreeing with everything she said.

Thankfully, inside the master bedroom, sounds faded to silence. Stillness surrounded me, and I pulled my jacket tighter across my body as the air pressure changed and a sadness hit me hard.

The room was just the way I remembered it from earlier in the day, only now the dim overhead bulb cast eerie shadows against the walls. The musty smell of damp cloyed my senses, and a draft from the open window whipped up.

The bedroom door blew closed with a slam.

I screamed—"What the...?"—and nearly jumped out of my skin, making a mental note that when I got to bed tonight, I was going to do my pelvic floor exercises.

Once I had my heartrate under control, I laughed at my silly overreaction and stepped across to the window, ready to pull it closed. I stopped short, taking a moment to enjoy the spectacular view. Westport spread out in front of me twinkling like fairy lights in an enchanted forest. The trees swayed in the breeze as the streetlights cast warm shadows against the pavement, and a deep contented sigh rattled my ribs pushing the sadness away.

Taking a deep breath and sucking the cool air deep into my

lungs, I looked down at the street noting the dark outline of a man standing alongside my car. Head bowed, his face was in darkness. A long coat covered his large frame as he lifted my windshield wiper and used it to secure something to my vehicle before he turned to face the house. The night protected his identity, but he looked straight up. He saluted me, the wind whipping his maniacal cackle upwards.

I gulped and slammed the window shut.

***

"Bob! Bob!" Taking the stairs two at a time, I knew I was being silly. The lone man could have been leaving me a welcome note for all I knew. Yet the whole incident left me cold, and even though I hardly knew Bob, the presence of another human being would make me feel a whole lot safer.

Upon reaching the ground floor, I saw the blonde had left as I scanned the hallway for signs of them. Bob's phone was lying on the floor behind the now closed door, yet he was nowhere to be seen. I moved into the lounge room, but Bob wasn't there either. A backdoor led off the kitchen—maybe he'd wandered outside.

The only sounds coming from within the house were my muffled footsteps on the boards and the occasional creak from the house as the wind whipped its walls.

"Bob! Are you there?"

Every scary movie I'd ever seen ran through my mind, and my pulse beat fast at my throat leaving me breathless.

"Stop it, Lizzie! You're being an idiot." I chastised myself, yet I was secretly happy to hear the sound of my voice filling the silence.

I smiled when I turned into the kitchen. The back door was indeed open. In a hurry, I stepped out onto the porch and tripped over something in the dark, stumbled and fell into the large, hard body of a stranger.

"Whoa!" he called, a hint of laughter in his tone as he helped steady me. His hold was firm, a little too firm, but I guessed he was just making sure that I was okay.

"I'm so sorry." I attempted to step away, yet the man kept his hold on me. "I didn't see that, that… what is that lying in the doorway?"

"It's my briefcase. I shouldn't have left it there. I apologize."

"No, I should have been looking where I was going. Instead, I was looking for the agent, Bob. Have you run into him?" I tried to pull my arm away as I peered into the darkness.

"He had to leave. I'm his replacement, Elijah." He released his hold on my arm and instead held his hand out for mine. The gesture was friendly, yet the slicked back hair and creepy smile did nothing to reassure me.

"Leave?"

"Yes. Urgent matter. I'm taking over the listing on the property from now on."

"But I was only going to be a few more minutes, and then I was going. Couldn't Bob have waited that long?" I shook my head, this making no sense to me. "And isn't that his phone inside the door?"

My gaze flipped from his face to his hand, wanting to slow my thoughts and get a grip on the situation. But the stranger near my car and the sudden disappearance of Bob accelerated my breathing and caused my thoughts to scatter. I felt wrong-footed.

"No, no. It's mine." Elijah dropped his hand, his smile frozen.

"But, but you're holding yours," I added, rubbing my chest to ease the tightness.

"Oh no. This is my private phone. The one you saw is my work phone." He shrugged like it was no big deal.

"Is Bob okay?" Feeling in my jacket pocket, I clasped onto my own phone and held it tight.

"Of course."

"Okay. Great. Well, I should get going too. My sister is waiting in the car for me."

"Is that your red Mini out the front? It's very cute." Elijah's eyes bored into mine as if he could see straight through my lie. "Before you go, Lizzie, I just need to get your phone number. Bob failed to take your details."

"Oh, of course." I rattled off my number, all the while searching my pockets for my car keys. When I left here, I wanted to do it quickly. "Umm, how did you know my name?" The cold air crept through my jacket as I shuffled from one foot to the other.

Elijah's jaw tensed. "Bob told me you were still upstairs."

That made sense. So why was the hair on the back of my neck tingling?

I said a quick goodbye and almost jogged to my car. Once inside I locked the doors, turned the radio to the happiest song I could find and sped away from the curb.

It was only as I turned off of May Street that I remembered the note from the stranger was still tucked under my windshield wiper.

CHAPTER 3

"What does it say?" Molly asked, her brows knitted together as she tucked her feet up under her.

The second that I'd made it to her place and told her about my stop at the house, she'd rung Danny, and we were now midway through a Zoom call.

"Yeah, reread it for us, will you, Lizzie?" Danny peered closer to the camera, his head looking larger than ever on Molly's laptop screen.

Unfolding the note, I turned it toward the computer camera. "It just says, *Stay away from the auction. Or else.*"

"Or else what?" Andrew asked, leaning over Danny's shoulder.

I shrugged.

"Who do you think left the note?" Molly asked.

I shrugged again.

"You should go to the police," said Andrew, concern etched into the deep lines on his forehead.

"And tell them what?"

"That the new agent is a weirdo!" added Danny.

"Yeah. What happened to Bob that he couldn't wait five more minutes?" Andrew asked.

"I hope it was nothing nasty." I chewed my thumbnail, worried about a man I hardly knew.

"What about the woman with the gorgeous shoes?" Molly asked. "Where did she go? Could she have been the one trying to get you to stay away?"

I shook my head. "It was definitely a man who left the note."

"She could have had a boyfriend," Molly added.

"I guess so."

"The neighbor looks suspicious," stated Danny.

"What makes you say that?"

"Have you seen her regrowth?"

"She *was* sneaking around looking in the windows when I got there," I recalled.

"I think it's the new agent," said Molly.

"Why would he want to scare away a prospective buyer? He'd only lose if the house didn't sell. I estimated his commission to be around twenty thousand dollars."

"Yes, but what if he was in cahoots with Lady Louboutin? He could get them the house at a great price and still get a good commission."

"I don't think it was he who left the note," I explained. "I know it was dark, and I was watching from a distance, but I think that guy was taller, and they were dressed differently. Elijah was wearing a Westport Property Sales jacket. I guess he could have thrown the coat on over it, but he would've needed super-human speed to beat me to the front door."

"What did you say that agent's name was?" Molly asked, her tablet in hand. "I'm going to look up the real estate company's website and see if he's legit."

"He just said his name was Elijah."

It only took a second before she frowned. "Westport Property Sales has no one by that name listed as an agent on their website."

"He could be new. They did have to replace Zac after all."

I was beginning to think Mum was right and the house had

bad karma. I mean, how many agents did it take to sell one old house?

"I'm sure I was just being silly," I added. "The house felt really weird in the silent night air. My imagination was running wild."

"You do have an overactive imagination," added Danny. "But you didn't imagine that note."

"I know. But I think that was just another buyer wanting to scare away the competition," I mumbled, distracted by the dinging of my phone's notifications. Those little icons were like an itch to me. They really bugged me until they were cleared so I allowed the conversation to drift into background while I checked it.

Hmmm, Facebook had a new friend request. Clicking on the screen, I squinted at the smiling face of Elijah.

"This is the guy!" I gasped, hurriedly turning my phone screen to face the camera.

"Why would he send you a friend request?" Molly recoiled slightly.

"That's very strange," added Andrew. "It's not common practice for an agent to send you a personal request like that. It's quite unprofessional."

"Is he cute?" Danny asked, as he moved closer to the camera.

Andrew rolled his eyes.

"No. He's kind of creepy."

"Ignore him," Molly demanded.

"But what if that affects my chances of getting the house?"

"How is it going to do that?" Her eyes narrowed as she assessed me.

"I don't know. I've never purchased a house before." I bit my lip as I considered the request.

Molly took my phone and peered at the screen. After a moment she said, "I know this guy. I went to school with him. His girlfriend is an investor. She has that show on television where you buy a house really cheap, renovate it in a week, then sell it super quickly and make lots of money."

"See! I bet that's the deal." Danny sat back and clapped his hands gleefully.

I huffed, defeat sitting heavy on my shoulders. "So, my chances of winning the bid are even less now."

"You won't bid any higher than you can afford, will you?" Andrew asked.

"Nope. Between my savings and what the bank will lend me, I have a very strict budget." And if I cut out my coffee habit, I could probably still afford to eat. Oh, who was I kidding? Life without coffee would just suck. "However, I'm willing to go to my max to get it."

"Scott just messaged you," added Molly, handing my phone back. "He wants to know where you left his dry cleaning?"

Bugger. I'd forgotten about that.

"Was it something he needed?" Andrew asked as I cringed.

"Just his favorite suit pants. I had a mishap and knocked his glass of red wine into his lap. He was pretty upset about it, so I said I'd get them dry cleaned."

"You should have just wiped it up for him." Danny grinned. "That would have made him happy."

Heat flushed my face. "Yeah, I tried that, but apparently they're Ralph Lauren, so nothing was distracting him." I shrugged as Molly sucked in a pained breath.

"You did take them to the cleaners, right?"

My blush deepened.

"Lizzie! Those pants will be ruined."

"I'll just buy him a new pair then." I had no idea what the big deal was.

"Do you know how much they cost?"

"They're pants. How much can they be?"

Molly opened Google and showed me the price tag.

"Whoa…" The world swayed and black dots appeared in my vision. At this rate I was going to have to give up more than just coffee if I ever wanted to afford this house.

Bugger.

CHAPTER 4

Nerves cramped my stomach and nausea swirled. Today was the day of the auction, and my sweaty palms were threatening to drown me. Twirling in front of the mirror, I took in my appearance, hoping I at least looked like a woman filled with confidence.

Before she left for work, Molly loaned me a dress that was nothing like I usually wore. It was crimson, skintight, and hovered just above my knee. For the first time I thought we actually looked alike.

She'd also loaned me some strappy high-heeled sandals, and I just hoped I didn't break my ankle before I even made it to the car.

I'd applied some shadow to my eyelids, upped the mascara, and added a slash of red to my lips. Danny had promised to do my hair before we headed to May Street, but as I checked my watch, I realized he was cutting it fine. My unruly mess took time to straighten, and time was not in his favor. I was just considering calling him to see where he was when my phone trilled.

"Danny, where are you?"

"Sorry, Lizzie. I've had an urgent treatment come in," he whispered. "This woman tried to perm her own hair, and the results are disastrous. I'm not going to make it in time." He sounded genuinely pained, but I wasn't sure if it was because he was letting me down or offended someone would do that to their own hair. Actually, I knew exactly what had upset him the most.

I sank back onto Molly's sumptuous mattress and picked at the skin around my fingernail, wondering if this was a tactic for Danny to stop me from buying the house.

"Who even has a perm these days?"

"Maureen apparently. I just don't know what on earth possessed her to attempt it herself."

"Can't Andrew do it instead?" I whined.

"Sorry, he has a doctor's appointment."

Disappointment pushed my butterflies aside. "I'll try Molly."

"Good luck. I'm pretty sure she has a client meeting this morning, and the client is super cute, so I doubt very much she'll postpone it to help you buy a crappy house."

I knew what Danny said was true, but I still had to give her a chance. After all she could have had a cancellation in her schedule and would now be free. However, as her phone rang out, my brow furrowed, and I allowed my shoulders to slump. Heaviness sat in my heart as I pressed my lips together and flopped back on the bed, staring up at the ceiling.

What was I going to do? Monday was Mum's day away from Grandma, doing her own running around, and God help anyone who interrupted that. Dad was taking a class at the Men's Shed. Molly was unavailable, and Danny had to restore some poor lady's self-esteem. That just left Scott.

I sat up and flipped my phone between my fingers. Scott didn't like to be interrupted at work, but on the off chance he was free he might still get here in time for the auction. And I did like the idea of him seeing the house before I purchased it. It may bring him around to my point of view.

Before I could talk myself out of it, I hit his number and chewed my lip waiting for him to answer.

"Elizabeth, you do know what time it is, don't you?" Irritation played in his tone.

"Hi, Scott. Sorry, have I called at a bad time?"

"It's Monday, and I'm at work."

"I kind of meant, did I interrupt a meeting or something?"

His long sigh made me cringe. "What can I do for you?"

"Well, today's the day of the auction, and I was wondering if there was a chance you could attend it with me."

"Have you spoken to my secretary about scheduling it in?"

I heard the distinct tapping of computer keys, and I could imagine the worried look in his soft grey eyes thinking he'd missed an appointment.

"No, of course I didn't speak to Belinda about it. I just had the thought that maybe you'd like to do this with me. We could go out and celebrate later today and you could stay the night." It had been a few weeks since we'd spent any quality time together, and I missed him.

"Elizabeth, you know how I feel about this. I understand why you want to move back to Westport, but you need to purchase a new build. Something that needs very little maintenance."

"But you should see this house," I whined.

"I've seen the photos. That was enough."

"They don't do it justice. If you walk through the halls, it'll enchant you."

"I very much doubt that."

Fair point. Scott did like things neat and tidy.

I released a deep sigh. "So does that mean you won't come with me?"

"I'm sorry, but I can't. I have a client meeting in a couple of minutes."

"All right. Well, thanks for the chat."

"Oh! Before you go, did the dry cleaners get the stain out of my Ralph Lauren trousers?"

I knew when it was time to end the call. "Sorry, Scott. I have another call coming in. I think it might be the office needing info about a client file I was finishing up. I've got to get it. Talk soon!'

I hit the *end call* button, and as silence reverberated back to me, I threw the phone on the bed and stretched my neck. I hated lying to Scott, but I had my fingers crossed so that made it okay, right?

The call left me out of sorts. Scott only had my best interests at heart, and I could see where he was coming from in regards to the new build. But I was determined to transform the house into a thing of beauty once again. Well, I personally couldn't do it but I had faith in the tradesmen that Google would find for me. I just had to get through the auction first.

With Scott out of the support equation that left me, myself, and I.

Could I do this alone? I wasn't known for the best decision making, but I had managed to survive city life for nearly ten years now. I'd also managed to build myself a fairly average career. Sure, I could have been far more successful, but the problem was I had never really wanted anything. Not *really* wanted it. Not like this.

Every time I thought about the house and the life I could build for myself there, my heart beat just that little bit faster, my breath quickened, and a yearning behind my breastbone pulsed. So, was I going to give it all up just because I had no one to hold my hand? No way. Not today.

The fluttery feeling in my chest was pushed aside by my accelerated heart rate as I pulled myself up to my full height and stood.

Slipping on the black jacket, I grabbed my handbag before throwing my phone into it and striding toward the door. I could do this, right? I could buy a house on my own. It couldn't be that hard. Didn't you just wave your paddle around whenever you wanted to make a bid? Even I could do that.

Feeling encouraged, I was about to pull the door open and make my way into the sunshine, when my phone trilled from the depths of the abyss, AKA my bag.

"Hello," I called after locating it among lost receipts and empty chocolate wrappers. How it had gotten that buried in such a short amount of time beat the heck out of me.

"Lizzie." Grandma Mabel's croaky voice echoed in my ear. "Danny just called me to ask about my night out with Eunice." She chuckled. "It was a hoot. We met the hot barman that Molly told us about, and a lovely group of young men even bought us drinks."

"Awesome."

"Yeah, it was great until Eunice had a wardrobe malfunction and we were asked to leave the premises. Just don't tell your mother about that bit, okay?"

"Umm, Grandma is there a point to this call?" I didn't want to be rude, but I also didn't have time to hear how her social life was better than mine.

"What? Oh, Danny's upset that he can't be with you today and asked me if I can take his place. I'd love to, but your mother's gone to get her tax done, and your father's not home. Can you come and pick me up?"

My sigh ruffled my hair.

"That was so nice of Danny." *Bloody brothers.* If he thought that having Grandma along for the ride would put me off, he had another think coming.

"Yeah. He's considerate like that. Now, can you come and get me? I heard that there's going to be a big crowd, and I want to get a good viewing spot. Since we're height challenged, we need to always be at the front or people won't see us."

That was true, and today of all days I did not want to be overlooked and not be visible to the auctioneer. "I'll be there in ten minutes."

Thankfully, Grandma was waiting at the door when I arrived, so all I had to do was help her into the car and then put her wheelie walker in the back.

"You look lovely," I commented, noting her knee-length black leather skirt that made her butt look non-existent, and the sparkly pink top accentuated the loose skin that once was an impressive cleavage. Thankfully, it was all hidden beneath her cable knit cardigan.

"I'm excited about this," Grandma proclaimed as I nosed the car in the direction of May Street. "It's not every day that I witness my granddaughter buy a house. And besides. I might just get on the news."

I jolted. "What? Why do you think you'll be on the news?"

"Because they were talking about this auction last night. It was one of those filler pieces. The reporter was saying how the house is cursed what with the first agent falling out of the window. Then that woman got run over out the front, and now the second agent has gone missing."

Pulling the car to a stop at the red light, I snapped my head toward her.

"Hang on. Bob's missing?"

"Apparently."

"But he was only at the house on Friday. True he left suddenly, but I never thought he was missing."

Grandma shrugged. "I'm just telling you what they said."

"Well, did they say what they think has happened to Bob? Did he go on holiday? Did he go mad? Get abducted by aliens?"

"All I know is that they said the house is cursed. But I think that will go in your favor. It should keep the sane people away."

"Are you saying I'm not sane?" The light turned green, and feeling slightly dizzy, I depressed the accelerator,

"You're as sane as I am, Lizzie."

Oh boy.

"Well, for what it's worth I don't think the house is cursed," I added, adamant. "I just think it needs someone to love it."

Grandma's teeth clunked as she swished them around. "I had a house like that once. It was the first house your grandad and I purchased. It was only tiny, but it fitted the two of us, and we were happy in it. It was our little love nest."

"That's so sweet. Do we have any photos of it? I can't recall ever seeing it."

"Nah. We couldn't afford a camera back then. Cute little thing it was, though."

"What happened to it? Did you outgrow it?"

"Termites ate the frame, and the roof fell in on us while we were sleeping."

Oh geez.

I gulped hard as the butterfly circus in my belly started an award-winning performance.

"Grandma, do you think I'm doing the right thing buying this house? Everything on paper says I should buy a new build. It would need no renovation, and I can move straight in." My voice cracked on the last word.

She reached across and touched my knee. "Lizzie, tell me why you love it."

Taking a deep breath, I attempted to convey my emotions. "I feel a kindred spirit with this property. It's like it's calling my name."

I expected Grandma to roll her eyes, but instead she nodded. "Then you need to buy it. The Universe wouldn't send it to you if it didn't have a purpose."

"I never pegged you to believe in that universe stuff." I smiled.

"I've learned a lot in my years, Lizzie. But the thing that stands out to me the most is never ever argue with the Universe. It knows what it's doing."

As I pulled the car to a stop outside the house in question and noted the crowd that had started to gather, I sure hoped it did.

———

"HI, BIANCA." My heels dug into the dirt when I stepped on to the remains of the front lawn. I raised a hand, shielding my eyes from the bright sunlight.

"Oh, hi. It's Lizzie, right?" She checked her tablet as her friendly smile radiated.

"That's me."

"Fantastic. Yes, I have it here that you're registered to bid today, which is excellent. I think we're going to have a good crowd, despite some of them being here out of morbid curiosity. I'm unsure whether the news piece last night was a hindrance or a blessing." Her nervous laugh quivered on the breeze.

"I just heard about that. What happened to Bob?"

She rolled her eyes so far into her head, I wondered if she were passing out. "What would I know? I'm just the assistant. All I know for sure is that I received a phone call on Friday night from him stating that he was quitting on the spot and I needed to get to the house ASAP."

"That's when he disappeared?" My mouth dropped open and a fly nearly buzzed in. Yeww.

"Yes. Ever since he took over from Zac he's not been coping with the stress of this house. We all thought he was going to have a weekend without a phone, but when his wife called us yesterday wondering when he was coming home from the retreat, we started to question what was really going on."

"I'm guessing there was no retreat."

"Nope." She frowned.

"So, Bob has gone, and not even his family knows where he went?"

Her silky-smooth hair tumbled around her shoulders as she

shook her head.

I bit my lip looking up at the house. "Did he say anything to Elijah before he left?"

"Nothing to indicate where he was going."

"Why did he leave mid-viewing?"

"I honestly have no idea. He just called me in a panic stating there was a prospective buyer in the house, and he had to leave immediately. I was to get there as quickly as I could, but one of my kids was feeling unwell, so I called Elijah and asked him to go instead."

"I think I was the person in the house, but if Bob needed to go so urgently, he could have just asked me to leave."

"Don't stress, Lizzie. Bob hasn't been his usual self lately. I'm sure when this auction is over, he'll come back with a smile on his face."

"Well… I guess if no one's worried then I shouldn't be either."

"Of course not! Bob's never been a fan of hard work. Thankfully, I have Elijah for that." Her grin was large and fast as we turned to look across the lawn at Elijah greeting some new bidders.

"He's really, umm, enthusiastic." I was going to say creepy, but that felt rude.

"That's one way to describe him." She beamed. "He just started with the company, and I don't think they knew what to do with him." Bianca shrugged. "He seems pretty interested in the house though, so that's a good start, right?"

As I scanned the crowd meandering around the grounds, my stomach cramped. "Are there many registered bidders today?"

"Not as many as we originally thought. Honestly, they're dropping like flies."

Well, that was kind of good news.

She went on. "Everyone's getting scared. They think the house is either cursed or haunted—which to be honest, if you're thinking that now, it's probably a good thing if you don't buy it."

My laugh danced on a ripple of nervous energy.

A vertical crease appeared between her brows as she bit her lip. "You don't believe in ghosts, do you?"

I shook my head before smiling at her. "Of course not!" If I didn't believe they were real then they couldn't visit me, right? "Nothing about this house scares me. I'm just hoping I win the bidding and it will be mine!"

Bianca blinked rapidly as she sucked in a fast breath. "Lizzie, you look like a lovely person. Are you sure this is the place for you?"

Not another doubter.

"It's fine Bianca. I know what I'm getting into."

"I don't think you do." She moved closer as she lowered her voice. "I shouldn't be telling you this, but this house has a lot of problems. You should consider staying away."

I laughed nervously. "You're the agent. You should be professing the benefits of purchasing it."

"I know I should. But I would hate for anything bad to happen to you."

"Why would it?"

"Because, well, look at everything that's happened so far. Wouldn't you be better off with a new build? I have a list of some gorgeous apartments overlooking the river."

If I heard that one more time...

"Thanks for your concern. But it's nothing a good saging won't fix." I laughed, only Bianca stared back at me blank-faced. "You know... when you light the sage and allow the smoke to banish the demons."

She shook her head. "Sorry, never heard of it. But honestly it doesn't sound like it will fix what's wrong with this place."

"It was a joke. Never mind. I might go for a quick look around the grounds before the auction starts." I wanted to distance myself from her before her nerves rubbed off on me and made me question my decision.

"Of course! You should check the outbuilding in the back yard. See what you're really signing up for." She looked at her watch. "We aren't scheduled to start for another fifteen minutes, so take your time."

She nodded toward the auctioneer as he chatted to the Westport Television News reporter. The last thing I wanted to do was be on the news. So I moved away from Bianca, my gaze falling to Grandma Mabel. I'd left her on one of the chairs set up under the large tree shading the front yard. She sat ramrod straight, her skirt showing more knee than I thought appropriate for an afternoon auction, and her smile was fixated on an elderly gentleman standing alongside the elegant blonde with the gorgeous Louboutins that I'd had a very intimate rendezvous with.

Grandma looked happy with her eye candy, so I headed for the side of the house, wanting to check out the building Bianca had referred to.

The garden was pretty sparse around the back, and even plants that had a strong will to live were mostly bare. Some I guessed were deciduous and affected by winter, but mostly they looked neglected.

That was fine by me. I wasn't much of a gardener, barely keeping a desk plant alive. But I was willing to give it a go. And surely, I couldn't make them look worse than they already did?

As I tiptoed across the dead lawn, attempting to keep Molly's heels from being ruined, I noted the designer suit-wearing agent pacing. The dust he was kicking up clouded the shine on his black leather shoes. He was in deep conversation on his cell phone with someone about bidding strategies and why they should bid more than they were proposing. I should have stayed close by and eavesdropped, but the decrepit building lurking in the back corner of the garden caught my attention.

As I walked toward it, I saw the suited agent glaring after me, and a shiver ran down my spine. Thank goodness a shrub next to the side entrance of the garage shielded me from his stare. Any longer under its rays and I would have withered, given up on the auction, and run for the hills. I didn't like conflict, and stopping someone else from reaching their dreams genuinely upset me, which was why purchasing via auction really wasn't my thing. But anything worthwhile never came easy, right?

Hiding behind the shrubbery, I swallowed hard, took a moment to gather my thoughts, and had a good look at the building. It was made of the same timber cladding as the house, but unlike the white house, it had been painted gray at some point in time. What the two buildings did share was that the paint was cracked and peeling, and the guttering looked a bit wonky. The side door was ajar, and it creaked and groaned as I pulled it back and stepped into the darkened interior.

Blinking, I allowed my eyes to adjust to the inside as I flipped my phone between my fingers, enjoying the texture and allowing it to soothe my nerves.

My footsteps disturbed years of dirt, and I coughed against the dust particles dancing in the beam of light. My gaze skimmed the room, but there wasn't a lot to see other than cobwebs, mouse dirt, and a snakeskin dangling precariously from the rafters.

I guessed this garage had never been built to house a car, more as a storage room slash workshop. But right now, the floor looked like it might just give way under my weight. I halted as the boards groaned.

Oh geez, what if I fell through the broken boards? Would anyone know I was stuck?

Oh yeah, Grandma Mabel would notice me missing.

Placing my hand over my racing heart, I slowed my breathing and stared up at the unpainted ceiling clearly seeing the water marks from years of the tin roof leaking. The cracked windows were opaque with dirt, and the walls leaned precariously to the left. No wonder Bianca thought I should run away.

Worried that at any minute the building could fall on my head, I took three steps backward, ready to make my escape and head back to the auction when something ginger and furry jumped out from the shadows. It hit me in the chest.

"Argh!" I squealed, tripping over my own feet and falling onto my backside. Dirt ground into the flesh on my outstretched hands. My phone smashed to the floor and skidded to a halt somewhere out of reach.

"What the heck!" I yelled, wondering if the pain shooting through my chest was actually a heart attack. Spinning on my bottom, I scowled at a fluffy ginger cat sauntering toward the door, seemingly happy with what he'd done.

It took a moment to regain control of my bladder, before struggling with Molly's strappy heels to get back onto my feet. She was going to kill me when she saw what I'd done to her dress. Rubbing my hands together, I tried to remove some of the dust before patting the dirt from my backside, and then searched for my phone. Thankfully it didn't take long to find it against the far wall.

As I hurriedly picked it up, I tapped the screen, waiting for it to illuminate, when my attention was grabbed by the creaking of the door behind me.

I jumped and pivoted, noting the shadow filling the door frame, the sunlight silhouetting the figure of a woman.

"Hello?" If I was this jumpy now, how was I going to cope if I won the auction and had to live here?

"Lizzie, there you are!" Bianca's voice was music to my ears. To be honest, the old garage had been giving off creepy vibes, and the hairs on the back of my neck stood to attention. "What are you doing? Is your phone okay?"

"A feral cat scared me, and I dropped it."

"Oh no, I hope you didn't break it."

I pushed the button to start it back up, quickly realizing that even though it lit up, the screen now held a million cracks and showed me nothing other than a white facade.

"I'm never that lucky." A deep sigh rattled my rib cage.

"That's such a shame." She pushed the door closed behind her, and the distinct sound of a lock clunking into place echoed through the gloom.

Well, that was weird.

"Umm, it doesn't matter," I replied, feeling wrong-footed. "I was due for a new one anyway. Do you have the time? I probably should be getting back to the auction."

"Oh sure. But don't worry, you've got ages before it starts. Oliver the auctioneer is caught up on the phone, so he'll start late. That's what I came to tell you."

I still didn't want to risk it. "I should check on Grandma too."

"She's fine. Busy chatting with Elijah." Bianca moved across the floor and into my personal space. "I wonder what this old building was used for."

"A workshop maybe."

"Possibly." She sighed, and an awkward silence filled the space between us.

"Well, maybe I'll go and find a seat before the auction starts. There's nothing to see out here anyway." I moved forward, ready to step around her, but was blocked as she changed direction and stopped in front of me.

I giggled and stepped to the right. She followed, and for a few moments we played the game of stepping into each other's path.

"I'm so sorry." I laughed again, taking a large step backward.

"It's no problem," she said, following me, her unsteady breath tickling my cheek.

"Umm, Bianca, what are you doing?" My stomach churned as my fingers began to tingle, and a buzzing sound started inside my head.

"Stalling for time."

"But I'm going to miss the auction."

"That's the point."

I instinctively backed up, hitting the wall behind me. "Why would you want to do that?" My tongue suddenly felt three sizes too big as all the saliva in my mouth dried up with my adrenaline spike.

"Because the man I work for wants this house for himself, and it's imperative no one stops that from happening."

"Westport Property Sales wants to buy it?" That made no sense at all.

"Of course not!" she snapped. "My other boss. He whom I shall not name." Her chuckle danced down my spine, causing some very unpleasant goosebumps to erupt.

"I'll give you your due though, Lizzie. You're persistent." When she glared down at me, I was suddenly aware how much taller she was. "I thought you'd back off after Zac fell out the window. I mean, the whole haunted house thing certainly put a handful of other buyers off."

"But… but Zac's fall was an accident. Why would that put me off?" I gulped as I tried to control my heart rate.

"It was no accident. He was pushed."

"You *pushed* Zac out the window?"

"No! What do you think I am? Some kind of monster? That was someone else's job."

My hand shook as my knees became rubbery, and I held the wall for support.

"Wow, your boss must really want this house," I whispered, scouring the room for exits.

It was her turn to sigh. "He does. Lord knows why, but my job is to ensure that he gets what he wants. You, however, seem the most persistent. I got that pesky neighbor to back off easily enough by reminding her of what happened to the previous owner."

"What did happen to the previous owner?" I swallowed against the tremble in my voice.

"Let's not get caught up on details, shall we. The point is you need to stay here until the auction is over."

"But…but…"

"But nothing. I don't like what's happening any more than you do, but we all do what we have to do, right?" She bounced on her feet, wringing her hands together as her gaze darted around me.

"What exactly is… umm… happening?"

"Nothing! Nothing is happening. That's the point. I don't want anything else happening. So please shut up and stay quiet, and this will all be over soon enough. Even though…" Her eyes looked wild and slightly deranged as they turned and locked onto mine. "When this auction is over you won't tell anyone that I stopped you buying it will you?"

"Umm…"

"Look, it was bad enough that I had to deal with Bob. I liked him, and I told him to stay away from this listing. There's plenty of other houses in Westport that he could have sold and left this all to me. But he wanted the commission. It's all he could think about."

"Deal with Bob? What happened to him exactly? Did you scare him away?" I needed a way out and inched along the wall until I was able to turn my body toward the door. Now, if only Bianca wouldn't notice.

She'd dropped her head into her hands and was rubbing her forehead furiously. "When I learned that Bob was showing the house to even more perspective buyers, I knew he had to be stopped. I called him Friday night and here he was—showing you and that blonde the house for a second time. I had to move to plan B. So, I called Elijah and said Bob had gone AWOL and he needed to be here to get both of you to leave. I didn't need to worry Elijah would accidentally do a good job and sell the house to you. Poor Elijah isn't that smart. The guy couldn't sell ice in a heat wave."

"But where is Bob now?" My blood pressure pulsed rapidly at my neck, and I shivered against the cold sweat dampening my brow.

"Nowhere you need to worry about. Life has been very stressful for Bob, and everyone will believe his suicide note."

"You *killed* him?" Stifling my scream, I edged slowly closer to the door.

"Well, no, not me per se. Like I said, that's someone else's job. Don't look so shocked. It was Bob's fault! He just wouldn't stop showing this house to more and more people! I told him to leave it alone. I had a buyer who would pay anything he needed to. What more did Bob want?"

I shrugged, stalling her until I figured a way out.

Bianca went on. "What he wanted was to see this house restored, and as you were the only registered bidder who wanted to do that, he was insisting you get a chance at winning the auction."

God love him. "How did you get him to leave?"

"I told him there was a break-in at the office, he was needed, and I was sending Elijah to take over for him. After that, my associate stepped in and finished the job. Look, I don't like it any more than you do, all right?"

"What about the blonde?" I croaked. "Looks like she'll stop at nothing to win the auction."

Bianca waved her hand dismissively. "She didn't raise the required capital and is no longer a threat. She's only here to spectate."

"There's still the suited agent. He looked pretty keen on winning for his client." I was now only a few feet from the doorway. All I needed to do was unlock it, run, and I'd be safe. Could I keep her distracted long enough?

Bianca laughed nervously. "His client is my boss. He didn't want to be here today, so he sent his representative. Of course, the client wants to follow along to ensure that the bidding *looks* legit. But if no one other than my colleague is there to bid, then my boss not only wins the property but gets it for an amazing price."

She had it all worked out.

"Why does he want this house so badly he would allow people to be killed for it? And why would you do that for him?"

Bianca paled and swayed on her heels. "He'll stop at nothing to get what he wants, Lizzie. Nothing!" Weariness pushed her bravado aside, and fear trembled in her voice. "I have no idea why he wants it, but if I don't succeed, my family is at stake."

"But killing someone?"

"I didn't kill anyone! I'm not like that. I've worked hard to get where I am today. I've always treated people with kindness, and I donate to the animal shelter. But when a man turns up at my daughter's day care and pretends to be her uncle, threatening me that next time he will take her and hurt her, I listen and do what I'm told. And all I did was arrange to have people in the right place at the right time." Fear pushed tears over Bianca's lashes, and she hurriedly swiped them away.

"You could have gone to the police and had them stopped."

"You have no idea who we're dealing with. They'll stop at nothing to get what they want. Which is why I need to keep you from bidding. Bloody hell, Lizzie! Why didn't you leave this all alone when my colleague left that note on your windshield? That tactic scared off three other bidders. Why not you?"

"I'm sorry," I croaked. "I should have taken notice."

"Yes! You should have. I quite like you, and it's really going to pain me to make this call." She swiped her phone open, ready to hit dial. I had no idea who she was calling, but I instinctively knew it wasn't going to end well for me.

"You don't need to do that! I'll leave and wipe this from my memory. There're plenty of other houses I can buy," I lied.

"Really?"

"Of course." I prayed my tone didn't sound as fake as my smile.

"Hmm, why don't I believe you? Maybe I should tie you up until my colleague gets here." She lowered the phone as her gaze swept the room. "Up the back. That looks like a good place to leave you."

I allowed her to take a few steps toward the destination before I diverted and ran for the door. My heart raced with every step, and adrenalin surged through my veins, but the heels slowed my movements and Bianca caught on a lot quicker than I'd hoped. She rushed toward me and grabbed my hair, pulling me deeper into the darkness. I screamed. She only released her hold when we reached the back wall and she grasped my shoulder, pushing me to the ground.

"That really hurt!" I cried.

"That's the least of my worries. Now stop your whining and sit still so I can tie you up."

Like that was going to happen. Scrambling to my knees, I attempted to crawl away from her. "You're a maniac and involved with killing people. You need to be stopped!"

"Yes, and once this damned auction is over, it will stop. I plan on taking my family and moving far, far away so that my boss can never find us again!"

Movement over Bianca's shoulder caught my attention, and as she scrambled through her bag, I allowed my gaze to stop on the side window.

I stifled a cry, relief flooding my body as Grandma's face filled the dirty glass.

Last year she'd had her cataracts fixed, and since then she had the distance vision of a hawk. Now, if only hawks could see through dirty glass into a darkened room and figure out their granddaughter needed help.

Unfortunately, it seemed they couldn't.

But Grandma's presence had alerted Bianca, and as she whirled to see what it was, I took full advantage of the situation, kicking the back of her knee.

She cried as it gave way, and she stumbled to stay upright.

However, I saw an opportunity and pushed up, launching myself at her, before knocking her to the ground.

She fell, her head hitting the boards with a loud crack as my full weight and momentum squashed her.

Hurriedly I rolled off, preparing my defenses, when I realized that she wasn't moving.

Oh my goodness! I hadn't killed her, had I?

I didn't wait to find out. Instead, I sprinted for the door as fast as a skintight dress and high heels would allow. Unlocking it, I stepped into the brilliant sunlight and blinked.

"What on earth is going on?" Grandma demanded, her teeth nearly popping out of her mouth.

My hand shook as I pulled the door closed behind me and fumbled to relock it from the outside. Only as I heard the clunk did I look at Grandma, before giving her a hug.

"You, you saved me." My voice shook, matching my knees as I gave Grandma the shortened version of events.

"I think I might have killed her." Tears welled behind my lashes, as Grandma Mabel moved past me and peered through the glass.

"Nah. I can see her twitching."

Oh, thank God.

"Now don't you worry about her," Grandma demanded, her thumb jabbing toward the door. "I'll keep guard here. The auction is about to start, and you need to get there. I'll call the police and tell them what's what."

I pulled her close for another hug. I didn't have a lot of time, and after everything that had happened, I wondered whether I should forget the auction and buy something else. But then an image of Bob ran through my mind, and Bianca's words played across it. Bob wanted the house to be restored, and even though I didn't know the details, he'd lost his life because of it. I owed it to him to at least try.

"Okay. But you have to come with me. I'm not leaving you

here in case she gets out and hurts you."

"All right. But you go ahead, and I'll follow as fast as my walker will allow."

"Promise?"

"I promise. Now get going or you'll miss out."

I kissed the papery skin on her cheek before giving her a weak smile. Adrenaline filled my veins as everything happened at speed, and I took off running toward the front of the house.

What I didn't anticipate was the suited agent, standing in the driveway, still talking on his phone. As we collided, his phone fell, getting lost in the jumble of gravel, Italian leather shoes, and Molly's stilettos.

It was only as the crunch of glass was drowned by his cursing that I realized my heel was wedged in the screen.

"I'm so sorry." Scrambling to remove it, I checked for damage, but quickly realized that spiked heels were lethal. "I'm so, so sorry."

He snatched the phone from me, calling me names I couldn't repeat.

"Don't you talk to my granddaughter like that!" Grandma yelled, as she marched across the grass. "She's a lady, and that's no way to speak to a lady. You need to learn some manners."

I probably did deserve a few of the words he'd chosen, but I got her point and loved that she was on my team no matter what.

Choosing not to hang around to watch the fallout, I slowed my pace and continued to the front of the house, just as the auctioneer announced the auction had started and asked for the first bid.

I pulled to a wobbly halt at the front of the crowd, noting the WTN reporter frowning at me and the blood trickling from my dirty, scraped knees. Ignoring it all, I closed my eyes, adjusted my dress, took a deep breath and raised my hand.

"WELL, THAT WAS AN EVENTFUL AFTERNOON," said Grandma as Constable Jonathan Smith of the Westport Police department pushed Bianca into the back of his patrol car.

Grandma had her fifteen minutes of fame as she recounted events to the WTN reporter, but she was now safely sitting on the seat of her walker, glaring at nosy neighbor Hazel staring over the fence.

"What happened to the real estate agent? You know, the one whose phone you broke?" Danny asked.

Once the auction was over and the police had arrived, I'd called him to come and get Grandma. Besides, he never would have forgiven me if he'd missed all the action.

I shrugged. "I saw him slinking off during the auction. If what Bianca told me is right, then if I were him, I'd be packing my bags and moving interstate. Their boss didn't sound like a nice guy."

"What about the man with the scar?"

I shook my head. "I didn't actually see him here today."

"So, do you think the house is really cursed? As the new owner you'd want to be sure that it's not," added Danny.

I still couldn't believe that I'd won the bidding, and that I now owned the house. Turning to admire it in the late afternoon light, I sighed contentedly.

"It's not cursed," I replied with a smile.

"Yeah, sure. Whatever gets you through the night. Now let's go and have a celebratory drink," called Danny, his grin large and fast.

"I'd love to join you, but I need to get home," said Grandma. "Your mother will be missing me, and I need to make a few calls. The girls from Bingo aren't going to believe it when they see me on the six o'clock news."

"Would you mind dropping her home?" I asked. "I'd like to stay here for a few more minutes. You know, just to soak it all in."

I wasn't allowed the keys until the bank had transferred the money and all the legal stuff had been processed, but the auctioneer had kindly told me that I could hang around for a while if I wanted to.

"All right. We'll meet you at the *Grinning Dog* in about half an hour."

I stood on the footpath and helped Grandma into the back of Danny's car, waving them goodbye until they disappeared down the street.

Only then did I turn to the house I now owned and released a gentle breath. Heat flushed my face as a delicious thrill flipped in my belly, and I leaned against the fence. *My* fence. It still didn't feel real.

Despite everything that had happened, I'd done it. I'd faced the day and all its challenges, and I'd won. I'd actually won! Maybe Grandma was right and the Universe really did know what it was doing.

I gave an excited squeal, enjoying the colors of the afternoon playing across the windowpanes and imagining everything this house would be.

"You won't be lonely anymore," I whispered to it. "You've got me now, and I'm going to ensure that you will be happy once again."

Only as the sun dipped below the rooflines, did I reluctantly move to my car, looking forward to an evening with my siblings and fantasizing about my new home.

I started the motor but froze as a shiver ran up my spine when a black Toyota silently pulled to a stop across the road, reminding me Bianca never did explain what happened to the previous owner, or why someone wanted the house so badly they would kill for it.

Dangerous Deeds

Lizzie ~ Book 1

DANGEROUS DEEDS - CHAPTER 1

It's probably important that I start this story by telling you who I am. My name is Lizzie Fuller and I'm the tallest female member of my family, measuring in at five feet two inches. I'm average weight with a small waist and hips. Unfortunately, I was at the front of the queue when God handed out breasts. I got my brown eyes and long dark, curly hair from my mum's side of the family. I also have dimples. I'm not sure who I inherited those from. Grandma Mabel was a bit of a wild card, so we don't really know what's hidden in that family gene pool. As far as intelligence goes, I'm not stupid, but I'm not a genius either.

Today I was debating that.

I was trying to turn the sticky lock preventing me from opening my new front door. Well, new was a stretch of the imagination, but it was new to me. So I guess it was okay for me to say that.

About a month ago, I had a premature mid-life crisis and realized that at the age of thirty-one, I didn't own anything of significance. Sure, I owned my car and a collection of high-end fragrances, but if I were to take an unscheduled trip to the Pearly

Gates, there was nothing to state this was who Lizzie Fuller was. True to form, I rushed out and bought a house. No time like the present, hey?

Now, I was wondering if I should have had an affair like every other sane member of society in the throes of a mid-life crisis. It would have been much easier… and cheaper.

"Hurry *up*. It's freezing out here," complained my sister, Molly.

Molly had come along today to help me move, but I was about to ask her what her definition of *help* was. So far, I'd yet to see it.

"It's stuck," I grumbled, rattling the door in the hope it would miraculously unlock itself.

"Use your shoulder," she suggested. "Give it a good shove."

The timber door looked pretty solid from where I was standing. "You're welcome to give it a go."

"Sure, but you're wearing jeans, whereas I'm in a skirt. Jeans are much more appropriate for the job."

I wasn't sure what occasion Molly had come dressed for today. It definitely wasn't moving house. Her skin-tight jumper, mini skirt, and high heeled boots looked amazing, but that was all they were good for.

Looking at the door again, I reached out and picked at the peeling paint, considering my options. I'd never rammed a door before, but maybe Molly was right—it just needed some encouragement. And the condition of the house was pretty decrepit so maybe the white ants might have weakened the frame for me.

"Stand back." I warned Molly before I changed my mind. Taking a couple of steps backward, I then ran at the door. My aim was perfect, my shoulder hitting the door above the lock. I'll admit to not being the strongest person on the planet, but I gave it my best shot. Unfortunately, the door was stronger than I was, and it held firm, causing me to bounce off it, landing on my butt on the timber boards of the porch.

Looking thoughtful, Molly stared down at me, hands on her

hips. "Maybe you should have just climbed the drainpipe and gone in through the open window up there," she said, nodding in the direction of an upstairs window.

"You couldn't have mentioned that before I threw myself at the door?" I snapped.

"I know you don't like heights."

I sighed and accepted her outstretched hand, getting back onto my feet and rubbing my shoulder as I moved.

Negotiating the couple of front steps, I stood on what was left of the front lawn, squinting up at the window Molly referred to.

She was right. The timber casement window was ajar.

"Why don't you climb it?" I asked. "You were good at scaling drainpipes when you were a teenager."

Her smile beamed at the memory before she looked down at her skirt and boots.

"What exactly did you come dressed for today?" I asked.

"Lizzie, it's important to always look your best."

I sighed.

"Come on, I'll tell you how to do it," she encouraged.

I knew it wasn't a good idea. I knew it. But I did it anyway.

"Take your shoes off," she suggested. "You get a better grip with your toes that way. Then you just grab the drainpipe and start to climb."

The window wasn't that high, and it was directly next to the drainpipe. So, if I didn't look down, surely I could do this.

Doing as Molly instructed, I kicked off my sneakers and started my ascent. The plumbing creaked and groaned, but before I knew it, I was nearly at the top.

Once the window was within reach, I stretched to grab it. The bolts holding the drainpipe to the wall didn't seem too happy with the extra strain put on them, and with an almighty snap they gave way, allowing the drainpipe to fall away from the building.

I screamed and held on to the rusted metal pipe with all my might.

Molly yelled, but I didn't hear a word of what she said. The only noises my brain received were the loud groan of the metal, the sound of rust flittering past my ears, and my blood pounding through my veins.

I said a quick prayer this would all end well, as the pipe gave its final groan and succumbed to my weight, plummeting to the ground with a mighty crash.

The descent had been much faster than the ascent, and as the air gushed from my lungs, I saw Molly's anxious face peer over me.

"Are you alive?" she cried. "Oh, please tell me that you're alive!"

I blinked.

As relief washed over her, she succumbed to an uncontrollable fit of giggles. By the time I had managed to roll over, push the rusty drainpipe off me, and sit up, she was on the grass next to me holding her sides as tears of laughter dripped off her chin.

"That was so not funny!" I cried.

"Oh yes it was. You should have seen your face."

Bloody sisters.

As I was considering if I'd actually broken any bones, a man walking his dog down the street, looked over the tiny fence toward us.

He gave me a small smile. "Afternoon, ladies. Is everything okay?"

Brushing the rust and grass off my top, I smiled back at him and explained I had just purchased the house and couldn't get in.

"Oh, well, I'm Edward. I live at the end of the street."

"Pleased to meet you."

"You should just go in the back door," he suggested. "It's never locked."

"Pardon?" I asked as the heat raced up my neck.

"The lock doesn't work on the back door, and the previous owner never bothered with it. Everyone on the street knew if they needed to get into her, that was the way to do it."

"Oh. Okay. Well...thanks then. I'll try that." Just why I hadn't thought to do that before listening to Molly's hare-brained ideas was beyond me.

WALKING through the knee-high grass toward the rear of the house, I struggled to remember what the hell possessed me to buy the very first property I'd seen. The house was a tiny, detached two-bedroom Victorian. Probably the best way to describe it was a dilapidated cross between a gingerbread house and the house of horrors. It was a money pit. I knew that. But my rival buyers wanted to knock it down, and I couldn't let that happen. All I saw were the memories the house would hold and knew that now was the time to protect it. It needed to be restored to its former glory. But why I thought I had the skills necessary to do such a thing was beyond me.

"Why didn't you buy one of those new apartments they've just finished overlooking the river?" complained Molly, looking around the overgrown yard.

To be honest, I was now wondering the same thing myself.

I pushed my hands deep into my pockets for warmth, and we walked to the back porch. The morning had started with the sun shining and not a cloud in the sky, but as the day had rolled on, the clouds had moved in, and the wind had picked up. Typical Westport weather.

I'd lived in Westport most of my life, only moving to the city ten years ago for work. But I'd had enough of working in the city, so I'd made a deal with my boss and would now be working from home.

I looked up at the old house and groaned. I really should have bought something with a usable office.

Reaching the rear timber deck, we negotiated the few steps. My first attempt to push the door open was unsuccessful, but with the use of my hip and a bit of force, we finally made it inside. Finding the light switch, I flicked it on and waited until the dim 60-watt bulb illuminated the room. I looked around and bit my lip. The excitement I'd felt when I awoke this morning was fading by the second. I surveyed the room, biting down on my disappointment. Molly followed me in. As she stomped her feet to warm herself up, I watched the dust rise and nearly consume her.

"Bloody *hell*." She coughed, waving her hand in front of her.

The smell of a stale, damp room hit me. I looked around at the dirty old kitchen cabinets and scarred timber flooring and felt a lump form in the back of my throat.

"Leave that door open, will you, Molly, and for goodness' sake, *stand still*."

Once the dust had settled, we silently walked through the house. I don't think either of us could find the right words to say. It was only as we were walking back down the stairs from the attic that Molly finally broke the silence.

"Who the hell thought this wallpaper was a good idea?"

It's funny, but I don't remember seeing the wallpaper the day I bought the house. To be honest, I don't remember the house looking this bad at all. That day, all I could think about was how it would look revamped.

The house had a simple floor plan. There was a main hallway with the staircase off the front door. To the right of the stairs was the lounge room and to the left was the kitchen. It's the same on the second floor, only to the right was my bedroom and to the left was the bathroom. The second set of stairs led to the attic, which was home to a second bedroom. The amount of work needed before this house was even liveable made me feel queasy.

The butterflies in my stomach were going crazy, telling me to run, but what the hell did they know? This was going to be fun, right?

"It's going to be great. A bit of a clean-up and you won't recognize it," I said, not daring to look Molly in the eye.

"A bulldozer would be better, but if you're insistent on sprucing it up, then you'll need a hot handyman to help you." Her petite nose wrinkled as she glanced around her. "What is that smell?"

"Rodents, I think." I blinked against the sting of tears. I hated rats. I mean, *really* hated them. Like phobia-hated them.

"Don't worry," said Molly. Sensing I was about to cry, she placed a hand on my shoulder. "The cat should help with that."

"What cat?" I looked at her, surprised. "I don't have a cat."

"Well, maybe he came with the house. When we walked in, he was sitting on the window seat in the lounge and looking quite comfortable, if I may say. Didn't you see it?"

"No. But there are a lot of things about this house I don't remember seeing," I said, feeling a weight on my chest. "How could I be this stupid, Molly?"

Molly pulled me into a big-sister hug. "You can come and stay with me if you like."

"Thanks, but no. I got myself into this, so I have to see it through," I said, sniffing. I took a minute to enjoy the warm, safe feeling of Molly's hug before I stepped back and pulled myself together. Feeling sorry for myself was not going to improve this situation. "Now, where was this cat?"

I followed Molly to the lounge, and there, sitting on the window seat, was a particularly large, fluffy ginger cat. Damn, she was right.

"But I don't want to own a cat," I whined, thinking I have trouble looking after myself. I should never be allowed to own any animal. You see, I did fish-sit for my mum once and—between you and me—the results were disastrous.

"I don't think you have much choice."

Okay, the cat did look quite at home sitting there, leg in the air, licking his privates. It stopped mid-lick, tongue sticking to its fur and gave us the once over. Deciding we were of no interest, it resumed what it was doing.

"Do you think it wants food, and then it'll disappear again?" I *was* hoping it had the wrong house.

"It's worth a try."

"There's enough bloody rodents around here it could have a smorgasbord." Maybe a cat wouldn't be a bad idea. This last thought was actually encouraging. I mean, a cat isn't like a dog, is it? You can forget to feed a cat and it will find food itself, won't it?

"I think you should go and get it some real cat food. It looks far too lazy to actually catch anything."

Bugger.

We spent the rest of the afternoon cleaning. Not that you could really tell where we'd been. The solicitor who'd handled the sale of the house told me it had been empty for about six months, and prior to that an elderly lady had lived there. I guess that explains the three inches of dust on every surface.

Molly helped a little in the end but not without complaints. By the time my dad arrived with the truck full of my belongings, we had dusted and vacuumed every inch downstairs. Now all I had to do was clean the bedroom and bathroom before I could go to bed tonight.

"Why don't you sleep at my place until you get this place straightened?" offered Molly.

"Thanks, but I'll see how I go. It's going to take forever to renovate this place, so I'll have to get used to it at some point."

"Yeah well, the offer stands. Even if it's midnight, just get in your car and head over."

I smiled. On the surface, Molly may look shallow and self-obsessed, but it was all an act. On the inside she's a big softy.

After Molly and Dad left, I improvised a lock on the back door by pushing a chair under the handle and made a quick trip to the local grocery store, which meant I could now feed not only myself, but also my squatter. I had a feeling Cat belonged with the house and that even after feeding him the best Kitty Kat food money could buy, he was not going anywhere. I'd also purchased every mousetrap and rattrap the store had in stock because my faith in Cat was pretty low. There was no way I wanted any of those little rodents crawling over me in my sleep.

Feeling tired and irritable, I drove back to my new home. I was exhausted, everything I owned was in boxes, and there was no way I was unpacking them until I knew all furry creatures had moved on. Most of the house was still filthy, I was responsible for a cat, and now the sun was setting, I was starting to feel Molly was right. I was pretty creeped out.

As I drove to the house, it looked dark, scary, and lonely. Carefully driving around the black sedan sitting opposite my driveway, I parked my car and contemplated spending the night in it. I could lock the doors and not have to face the house until morning when it was bright and sunny again.

But no, I had to stop being stupid and get inside. There was nothing in there that could hurt me. I had personally checked every cupboard for dead bodies and scary creatures earlier in the day. Checking again would probably put my mind at ease, but there was no freaking way I was doing that in the dark.

Entering the house, I turned on every light in every room, all except the attic which—as that particular light switch was at the top of the stairs—was way too creepy for me to even think about.

I stood outside my bedroom door and looked toward the darkened staircase, terrified. I probably should have ventured up there and turned it on. Peace of mind is a powerful thing. Oh well, I'll just lock the door, jump into bed, and pull the covers over my head. That would work just as well.

I'D BEEN DREAMING. Someone was standing over me, watching me while I slept. It wasn't a reassuring, angel-watching-you kind of dream. It was a scary, some-lunatic-wants-to-kill-you kind of dream.

I woke with a start.

The hair on my arms and back of my neck stood on end as I sat up and had a good look around. Everything was the way I'd left it—everything *except* the bedroom door. It was now wide open, swinging on its hinge…

Would you like to know what happens next? Then check out *Dangerous Deeds*.
Find your copy here

WHEN ONE DOOR CLOSES, another opens...or falls off its hinges.

They say that love is blind. Sure, they weren't necessarily talking about old houses at the time, but that's the story that Lizzie is sticking with. And she likes that theory a whole lot better than the one about her losing her mind.

She knew that buying a fixer upper meant stumbling into an unknown abyss of demolition, dust and unfathomable costs, but she never expected to find an engagement ring and letters of forbidden love hidden under the attic floorboards. Nor did she expect the lazy cat, or the drop-dead gorgeous handyman. And she definitely didn't predict the stalker.

As the renovation begins and the house starts to slowly return to its former glory, the letters dog her dreams. Who is the mysterious penman? Why was their love forbidden? And who is trying so hard to keep her from learning the truth about it all?

Working alongside her hunky handyman is proving to be

quite the distraction, but Lizzie is determined to solve the puzzle of the long-lost love affair. But can she restore the house to its former glory, and solve the mystery before her stalker catches up with her? Or will she lose everything... including her life?

Find out in this spellbinding romantic cozy mystery where hearts, along with homes, receive the renovation of a lifetime.

DANGEROUS DEEDS IS the first cozy tale in The Westport Mysteries series. If you like handy heartthrobs, suspenseful puzzles, and quirky characters, then you'll adore Beth Prentice's charming story.

Find your copy here